# OUR SUPERPOWERS

### Celebrating Differently-Abled Kids and their Siblings

Discover how interacting and connecting with differently-abled kids can lead children and adults to tap into superpowers they never knew they had.

CHRISTINE L'ABBÉ
ART BY iCENIZAL

Our Superpowers
Copyright © 2022 by Christine L'Abbé

All rights reserved. No part of this publication may be reproduced, distributed, or transmitted in any form or by any means, including photocopying, recording, or other electronic or mechanical methods, without the prior written permission of the author, except in the case of brief quotations embodied in critical reviews and certain other non-commercial uses permitted by copyright law.

Tellwell Talent
www.tellwell.ca

ISBN
978-0-2288-6121-8 (Hardcover)
978-0-2288-6120-1 (Paperback)

*To my greatest teachers Juliana and Gabriela, and to all the differently-abled children I have had the privilege to cross paths with.*

Excited by her dream, Juliana ran into the kitchen to find her mother and sister, Gabi.

"Mama, Gabi! My heart is so happy. I dreamed that I had a horse ranch with foals!"

"Oh, how beautiful, my love," Mama responded. "Would you like to go to Calabogie Ranch today? We could see real horses there and perhaps learn how to care for them. I bet Gabi would love it, too."

As the words 'real horses' escaped Mama's lips, Gabi began to kick her feet, pulling her top lip down to communicate her joy and enthusiasm.

That afternoon, they embarked on a journey to Calabogie Ranch. Juliana and Gabi sat in the back of the van, side by side.

They drove down a long road surrounded by trees with pink blossoms.

Gabi looked out the window with focused attention, eyes wide, mesmerized.

Juliana, who understands her differently-abled sister's way of communicating, agreed. "I like the pink trees too, Gabi," she said.

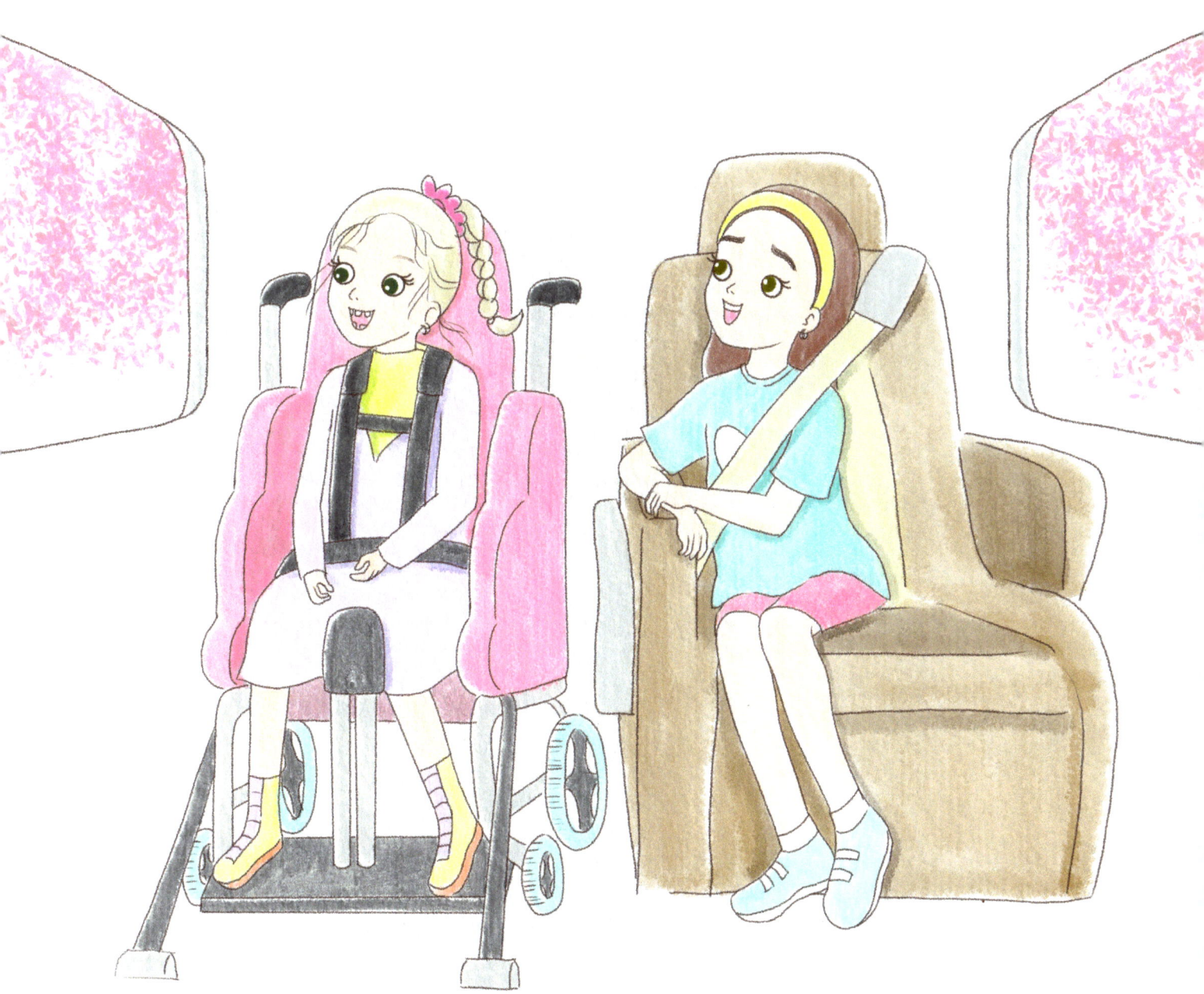

Gabi, feeling seen and heard, turned to her sister to exchange a deep affectionate gaze – one that Juliana knew meant "I love you" in Gabi's language.

As Gabi stared into her eyes, Juliana felt her heart expand with love.

Juliana often shared with Mama that gazing into Gabi's eyes made her feel happy and bright. Juliana loved when her sister gave her "I love you" eyes.

Juliana and Gabi were masterful at connecting without needing to say or do anything.

They could sit together in silence. In peaceful appreciation of one another.

Juliana always saw Gabi as whole.

At gymnastics, the girls huddled around Gabi, curious. Juliana was proud to introduce Gabi to her friends and include her in conversations so that others could see her sister like she did.

Juliana asked her sister for her opinion sometimes: did she prefer her pink gymnastics suit or her blue one? Gabi always chose pink, or whatever glittered most.

Even though no words were exchanged, Juliana always understood what Gabi wished to communicate.

When Gabi was sad, she looked away and engaged less with those trying to speak to her.

When Gabi was happy, she kicked her feet, pulled her lip down, and opened her eyes wide.

Juliana even intuitively knew when Gabi needed snuggles. "I love you" eyes were a sure sign.

When the family arrived at the ranch, they followed a path to the main entrance to meet Mr. Rogers, the head rancher.

As Juliana and Mama walked along the path, Gabi riding along in her chair, they took in their surroundings, connecting with the trees and the sounds that enveloped them.

They delighted at the heat of the sun on their faces, and embraced the breeze of the wind as it rippled through their wavy hair.

Gabi's pace and different ways of communicating taught Juliana and Mama to slow down, become curious, observe, feel, and listen with all their senses.

Seeing the world through Gabi's eyes helped Juliana and Mama appreciate the ordinary and be present to all that is.

As they arrived at the entrance to the ranch, Juliana spotted another child. She walked towards him to introduce herself.

Andrew was seated on a rock near the ranch entrance. Juliana sat beside him and said hello. But the boy didn't say anything back.

Juliana could sense Andrew didn't want to talk. So she said, "I like to just sit with my friends sometimes, too." The boy moved his body forward and back, shaking his hands slightly and making sounds without looking at Juliana. Andrew was happy and Juliana could feel it.

Juliana was always drawn to children who were not like everyone else because she could feel just how special they were inside.

She often shared with Mama that she struggled to connect with some of the other children at school in the same way she did with kids like Gabi and Andrew.

"Nobody makes my heart tingle the way they do," she shared.

Mama reminded Juliana that ALL children are unique and special, just like Gabi and Andrew.

"All children's hearts can shine brightly when they are free to share their unique abilities with others, but sometimes we forget that our superpowers live inside of us, not outside of us," she said.

"Superpowers are not limited to what we do and what others can see. Our superpower is the unique combination that makes us exactly who we are. Those things that make us and our lives different. The different ways we think, create, play and see things," she continued.

Juliana, Gabi, and Mama slowly made their way towards Mr. Rogers, who stood near the paddock.

As they approached, Juliana noticed a beautiful brown horse galloping free on the other side of the fence.

She approached gently, quietly, hoping the horse might come say hello.

"What a beautiful horse," said Mama to Mr. Rogers.

"Yes, Rose is a beauty. But she's wild. Nobody has been able to go anywhere near her," Mr. Rogers explained.

To Mr. Rogers's surprise, the horse slowly made her way towards Juliana, coming close enough to allow Juliana to stroke her muzzle.

Mr. Rogers was shocked.

"Oh my, your daughter must have superpowers! That horse has never allowed any of us to touch her."

Mama smiled. "Why yes. She has developed a superpower that allows her to use all of her senses to be present. This helps her connect and communicate so others can feel safe when they are with her. Juliana feels deeply and can attune to just about any live creature. She learned this through her deep connection with her sister, Gabi, who is non-verbal," she said.

Juliana listened intently to her mother's words.

Her heart expanded with light and love. She felt so special.

In that moment, Juliana realized that Mama was right; she did have superpowers!

She also realized she was lucky to have a sister like Gabi.

Juliana ran towards Gabi. "I'm so happy to be your sister, Gabi – we have superpowers!" she whispered in her ear.

Gabi kicked her feet and smiled. Juliana knew Gabi felt loved and seen for her uniqueness.

Juliana rolled her sister's wheelchair towards Rose. She also wanted to give Gabi a chance to connect with the horse through a shared gaze, a heart connection, and physical touch.

Excited, Mr. Rogers asked if Juliana could visit again to help out on the ranch. He wanted Juliana to come back so she could further tap into her superpower of connecting with the horses.

On the drive home, Gabi slept peacefully while Juliana daydreamed about all the things she could do with her superpowers.

What are your superpowers? What is different about you and your life? How do your superpowers make you special?

## AUTHOR'S NOTE

Developing a connection with a differently-abled child offers many gifts. It can: awaken and activate all of our senses; foster a deeper connection with ourselves and others; encourage us to be true to who we are rather than trying to fit into a mould; help us understand the importance of celebrating differences to learn about ourselves and others; empower us to recognize that everyone plays an important role; show us that we can co-create and shine our unique light, even as a collective; and so much more.

Opening to these gifts is an invitation to connect to a person's essence, a force that is expansive and free, extending far beyond the realm of what is readily visible on the outside.

We are often taught that children with special needs or disabilities are not as intelligent or capable as their neurotypical peers. But that simply isn't true.

Our idea of what it means to be intelligent is limited.

Intelligence extends way beyond physical and cognitive abilities. What about creative intelligence? What about emotional and heart intelligence? What about sensory intelligence? What about levels of intelligence that we simply haven't yet tapped into or developed the language for? Children in our society are evaluated from a very limited lens compared to what is actually possible. This narrow view limits their capacity to truly explore, discover, and express their innate potential.

Unlike neurotypical children, our neurodiverse children are un-mouldable. They have a greater capacity to remain authentic, whole, pure, untainted, true, and shine their unique light. Because they are incapable of being any other way, they can arguably experience greater joy than our neurotypical children, who learn early on that they must abandon parts of themselves to survive and fit into society.

Imagine a world where all of our children find joy in their ability to simply 'be' without feeling societal pressures to 'do' in order to be seen, acknowledged, and validated. In this world, all children feel they are enough, that they are lovable. If all children were seen, heard, and valued in 'being', there would be no distinction between a neurodiverse and a neurotypical child. All children would simply be children.

Imagine a world where children are led to explore their uniqueness, cultivate their inner world, and celebrate each others' differences. A world where children learn from each other through the lens of love and curiosity rather than judgment.

If our children were taught to embrace their quirks and encouraged to find their special something rather than inherit stories, ideals, and scripts about how they should be that simply don't fit, wouldn't the world be a kinder, more loving place?

Our neurodiverse children are here to teach us. They are here to model presence, authentic connection, and unconditional love. To guide us back home to ourselves. To love, purity, kindness, compassion, and empathy. To our gifts and innate abilities. They are here to lead us to deeper sensory awareness and a more vibrant connection to ourselves, which paves the way for us to walk a life more fully aligned with our soul, our inner truth.

It is only after we have found the courage to open up, see, and receive the gift being offered to us that the magnificence these beautiful children are here to share will become visible to us. Why? Because the act of learning to see ourselves in our true, authentic light grants us the clarity to experience all of life through the lens of truth, through the lens of love.

*Our Superpowers: Celebrating Differently-Abled Kids and their Siblings* is a story about the unique opportunity available to siblings of differently-abled children (and anyone else who is lucky enough to cross their path).

**Bringing Authentic Connection to Life at Home, at School and in Therapy**

**Exercise 1:** Sit in a circle with friends, classmates, family, or others in your community. Close your eyes and practice sharing what you feel in each other's presence. Allow yourself to be free to express whatever comes up.

**Exercise 2:** Sit across from a non-verbal child. If they are willing, practice gazing into their eyes to connect with them. Allow yourself to listen to the words that pop into your mind. As you connect, try to feel what comes to the surface and name it. If you are doing this exercise with your children (or students), approach it in a fun and playful way.

**Exercise 3:** Sit with a non-verbal child, side by side. If they are willing, hold their hand and close your eyes. Focus on your heart centre. Feel. Name what comes to the surface.

These exercises ask us to step into a differently-abled child's world, learning to listen and communicate in new ways while deepening the connection to ourselves. Remember, the more you practice, the more you will tap into your innate ability to connect with others on a deeper level. It's all about trusting ourselves and inviting freedom of expression.

### How to Speak to Your Children About Children Who are Different

The most straightforward way to help your children understand how to be in a relationship with differently-abled children is to teach them a simple truth: each one of us is whole, perfect, and complete. We shine our brightest light when we are free to be exactly who we are. We are most happy when we can pursue what we are innately good at, what we are naturally drawn to. To do this, we need room to explore, play, and be free to try different avenues. The same applies to our children.

You can begin by making small verbal and non-verbal communication shifts in your parenting such as embracing differences, celebrating uniqueness, and cultivating your child's authentic self. These subtle changes alone will give you new insights about how you can begin to teach your children about differently-abled children in ways that are authentic to you and your family.

And remember that our children observe our every move – we are the example. So by allowing ourselves to choose a path that aligns with our own authenticity, our soul, we automatically grant our children permission to do the same.

Finally, when you can clearly see your own magnificence, you will learn to see your children and differently-abled children through new eyes, and naturally begin to observe their inherent gifts. Only then will you develop the capacity to communicate with your children about the new, more expansive forms of intelligence you feel emanating from the differently-abled children you meet.

### How to Interact with Differently-Abled Kids

Be curious about who they are and their differences
Be kind with your words and actions
Be love with your energy
Be open to superpowers in all forms (big and small)

Take the time to hold their hand. Look into their eyes. Or simply practice sitting with them in silence. Allow yourself and your kids to absorb their presence. To pause. To simply 'BE' with them. Then try, just for a moment, to see the world through their eyes.

Evolve Movement Co-Founder and CEO Christine L'Abbé is a fierce advocate for families with differently-abled children, and she has a clear vision for a new model of care that is based on strengths, not limitations. Her work is bringing to life an alternative model of care that Christine and her colleagues call a Holistic Family Healing Approach.

Because of her own experiences with her daughter with Atypical Rett Syndrome, Christine is passionate about using education to empower other families like hers. As a pediatric Anat Baniel Method® NeuroMovement® practitioner, Christine sees perfection in every differently-abled child she meets. And she wants every parent to receive support in healing from their own trauma so they can foster the healthy development of their differently-abled children and their siblings.

CPSIA information can be obtained
at www.ICGtesting.com
Printed in the USA
BVHW022305091122
651633BV00002B/34